FROST

www.hollywebbanimalstories.com

STRIPES PUBLISHING LTD
An imprint of the Little Tiger Group
1 Coda Studios, 189 Munster Road,
London SW6 6AW

This hardback edition first published
in Great Britain in 2018

ISBN: 978-1-84715-953-3

A CIP catalogue record for this book
is available from the British Library.

Printed and bound in the UK.

2 4 6 8 10 9 7 5 3 1

HOLLY WEBB

FROST

stripes

For everyone who has written
to me asking for a fox book!

~ HOLLY WEBB

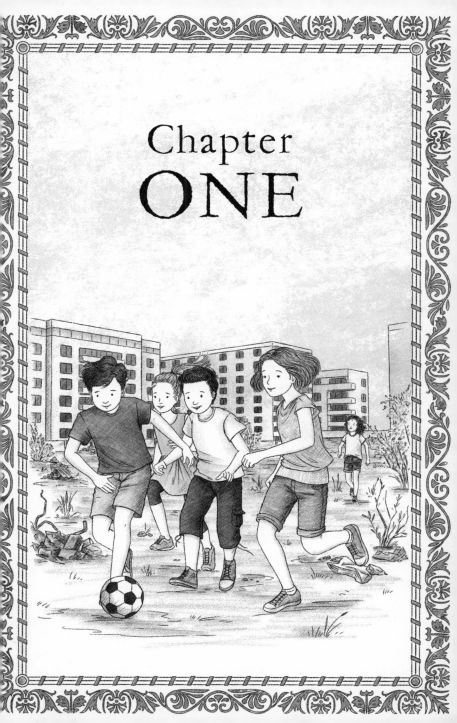

Chapter ONE

"Wait for me!"

But they didn't. They never did wait. Cassie kept on calling, just in case. It wasn't even as though she was the youngest of the kids from their flats but William always called her his "baby sister", so everyone thought she was the babyish one. She watched the rest of the children disappear over the patch of wild ground, kicking a ball back and forth between them.

"Didn't want to play football anyway," she muttered to no one, as their shouts died away. It was almost true. She didn't much like football, but she would have played if they'd let her, because she didn't want to be on her own.

Cassie slumped down on an old tyre that someone had dumped among the patches of foxgloves and picked a pink spotted flower from one of the tall stems. She slipped the tiny bell over her finger and stroked it. It was soft, almost sticky, but very smooth. "You wouldn't fit a fox," she whispered. "Not even a little one."

She only just saw it – the faintest twitch out of the corner of her eye. A movement in the tall plants. Something was there, watching her. It was probably a cat, but then there were sometimes stray dogs around too... Cassie swallowed, wondering if she should shout for William. He was supposed to be looking after her – Mum always reminded him when they went to play outside. If she yelled, he'd have to come, wouldn't he?

"I can see you," she said, trying not to let her voice squeak. "I know you're there!"

She glared fiercely at the foxgloves and saw them shiver a little. A dark nose appeared between the flowers and then a sandy-whitish muzzle.

Cassie stopped worrying about a fierce stray dog and leaned slowly forward, holding her breath. There was a fox in her foxgloves!

The fox stared back, just as surprised and curious as she was, Cassie thought. Its ears were huge and they twitched as it peered inquisitively at Cassie.

She knew that there were foxes on the waste ground, of course she did. Mum and everyone else at the school gates complained about them. They said there was always fox poo in the playground, and that foxes got in the litter bins and spread mess everywhere. They shrieked and squealed in the night too, like little ghosts. Mum talked about the foxes as if they were nasty, dirty things. Cassie had seen them occasionally as they walked back from the bus stop in the dark – a fox might skulk past into the shadows, faded to grey by the lamplight. London was full of them, her dad said, even though they were meant to be countryside animals.

This fox was beautiful. It was small, but not skinny and greyish-red like the ones she'd seen before. Its fur was really red – a rich, orangey red-brown that glowed against the leaves. It edged a little closer to Cassie, pushing its way through the tall foxgloves, and she saw that it had neat dark socks and a white front and chin like a cat.

The fox gazed at Cassie with maple-syrup eyes and then stared hopefully at

Cassie's bulging pocket. Cassie glanced down too, then looked back at the fox, frowning. "Biscuits?" she whispered. "I don't think foxes eat biscuits."

Then again, she thought, they were a sort of dog, weren't they? Her cousin Riley's dog ate everything. He'd snatched a biscuit right out of Cassie's hand once, and he'd definitely eat these. Mum had given her the end of a packet of ginger biscuits for a snack, her favourite. Cassie pulled one out of the wrapper and saw the fox's ears swivel eagerly as it tracked the rustling sound.

"You do want one, don't you?" Cassie stifled a laugh – she didn't want to scare the fox away. "OK. One for you, one for me?" She reached forward and put the biscuit down on the worn path through the grass.

The fox looked at it, and then at Cassie, and then it darted over, snapping at the biscuit and tossing it up into the air. It caught the treat neatly in its jaws, then whisked away, tail held proudly high.

Cassie watched that tail, tipped in white, until it disappeared among a tangle of bramble bushes.

After that, Cassie stopped asking to join in when William and the others went off to play football. She spent the summer holidays watching the foxes. There was a whole litter of them, she discovered, with a den somewhere deep in the bushes. Four cubs and their mum and dad – though Cassie hardly ever saw the adult foxes since they were much shyer than their babies.

They were her secret. Cassie kept expecting William or one of the others to notice the cubs – to tell their own story about feeding a little fox cheese and onion crisps – but they never did. Perhaps they just weren't looking, Cassie thought, or else they were too loud when they went rushing by.

The little fox with the white tail tip brought the other three cubs to see Cassie but they were never quite as brave as she was. Cassie had decided that her fox was a girl. She didn't really know for sure but she wanted her to be. She was fed up with William teasing her and her baby brother Lucas making Mum so tired all the time. She wanted another girl around. In her head, she called the fox cub Frost, because her white tail looked like the frost patterns on the leaves on the coldest morning, an icing-sugar sparkle.

The other cubs only peered through the foxgloves at Cassie, whiskers twitching.

They never came to beg for snacks like their sister but they were so funny. The four of them were like puppies, she thought. Or toddlers. Always rolling around on top of each other and snatching each other's toys. One of the cubs only had to find a particularly exciting twig for the rest of them to decide it was definitely theirs and start a full-on wrestling match.

Cassie never went near their den. She wasn't sure she'd be able to, anyway, because she had a feeling it was right in the middle of a fierce clump of brambles. But if she threaded her way through the weeds and sat looking at the scrubby stretch of dry grass by the bramble patch, the fox cubs were happy enough to pretend she wasn't there.

They seemed to get bigger so quickly
and they changed so much. The first time
Cassie had seen the little fox with the
white tail tip, she was still darkish brown
and fluffy along her back and her tail –
her baby coat. But a week later Frost's
coat was all red and Cassie was sure she'd
grown. Her ears looked sharper and her
nose was definitely more pointy.

By the end of the summer, around the time Cassie's mum was muttering about getting new school shoes, the cubs looked almost like grown-up foxes. The white tip at the end of Frost's tail was an even brighter white, as though she'd dipped it in paint. She wasn't tame, exactly – she wouldn't come close enough to be stroked – but she was almost friendly. And she definitely liked Cassie's snacks.

"It'll be quieter for you when everyone's back at school," Cassie murmured. She passed the fox cub a cube of cheese, and Frost sniffed at it suspiciously and then gulped it down. "But I'll come and see you after school instead."

Actually, Cassie had noticed that the fox cubs were asleep for most of the day now anyway. They seemed to come out in the early evening – after tea, when Cassie's mum was trying to get Lucas to go to sleep. Every so often she saw them in the daytime still, but in the evenings they came yipping and scuffling out of their secret den and played.

Once or twice, when she'd woken up early in the morning and gone to look out of the window of the flat, Cassie had seen the cubs sniffing eagerly through the bushes. They did ballet leaps, jumping to catch something – she wasn't sure what. Mice, maybe, or beetles? The book she'd got out of the library said that foxes even ate worms.

They definitely ate the late summer blackberries. Cassie had watched them do it, gently nipping the berries off the brambles with their teeth. The cubs tried to stand on their hind paws to reach the fruit but they couldn't get all of them. Cassie had never liked blackberries much herself – too sour and too seedy – but she could reach higher than the foxes could. So after that, she picked them for the foxes, leaving little piles of blackberries balanced on dock leaves at the edge of the grass. They were never there the next time Cassie looked, and she knew the cubs had eaten them because their poo turned purple and once she accidentally trod in some. It took ages to get it off her trainer.

Even though she'd wiped away as much as she could, Mum still noticed when Cassie came in later. She said it stank and Cassie supposed that she was right, but somehow she didn't mind as much as Mum did. It just made her want to laugh, thinking of the foxes nibbling blackberries so carefully. She wondered if they got purple juice down their white chins. They must have eaten an awful lot of blackberries for it to go right through them like that.

The blackberries on the bushes were all gone by the week that Cassie went back to school and Cassie wondered if Frost missed them. On Friday afternoon she ran ahead of William and her mum, who was pushing Lucas in his buggy. And instead of going along the path to the main doors of their flats, she darted round the back of the block to the waste ground. She'd saved the apple from her packed lunch and she left it by the bramble patch for the foxes. She wondered if Frost had ever seen one before.

"You shouldn't feed them," someone said snappishly as she raced back round the side of the building to see where Mum and William had got to.

Cassie pulled up short and saw Mrs Morris sitting on a bench outside the main doors. She looked out of breath and cross, and she was glaring at Cassie.

Mrs Morris lived in the flat next door and she was always complaining to Mum about Lucas crying. Mum said she didn't mean to be horrible, and she was probably not feeling well or perhaps she was lonely. But Cassie had heard Mum muttering under her breath about Mrs Morris when she thought Cassie and William weren't listening. Cassie's dad wouldn't go out into the hallway if Mrs Morris was there because he said she'd moan at him for at least ten minutes if she saw him.

"Wh-what did you say?" Cassie stammered. How did Mrs Morris know she'd been feeding the foxes? Had she seen Cassie from her balcony?

"You're just encouraging them! Nasty, dirty creatures. They make such a mess – they've ripped open those bin bags someone left by the wheelie bins again. There's rubbish everywhere!"

"What's the matter?" Cassie's mum came hurrying up, shoving the pushchair in front of her so that it bumped over the paving slabs and Lucas whined. "Cassie, you shouldn't run off like that. I didn't know where you were. What's going on?" she added sharply.

"Your little girl keeps feeding the foxes on that patch of waste ground." Mrs Morris pulled herself up from the bench with an effort. "You should keep a better eye on her! She'll probably catch something – those creatures are filthy."

Cassie could see that her mum was

furious but she smiled at Mrs Morris, a thin smile that stretched round her teeth. "Thank you. I'll talk to her. Cassie, William, upstairs now." She marched away, with Cassie trailing after her to the lifts.

"Is that true?" she hissed at Cassie as the doors wheezed shut. "Have you been hanging about round there? You know I told you only to play on the swings and the slide!"

Cassie looked sideways at William and he glared at her. They hardly ever went to the little playground at the front of the block. It was full of baby stuff, more for toddlers like Lucas than for them. There was a patch of tarmac that was OK for football, it even had a goal marked out, but there were always older kids playing on it. Everyone their age went round to the waste ground. But if Cassie told her mum that, she'd get William in trouble too. Her mum hated the way the waste ground was full of rubbish, she said it was dangerous. If Cassie said they all hung around there they'd never be allowed to play outside, not without an adult watching over them. She scowled at William and kicked gently at the side of the lift.

"Sometimes I go down there," she muttered. "Not all the time."

"She's usually with me and Sam and the others," William agreed, trying to look like a reliable big brother.

"Well, keep an eye on her! It's bad enough Mrs Morris having a go, let alone that she's actually right!" Her mum let out a sigh. "Don't go round there again,

Cassie," she added in a gentler voice. "It's not a good idea. Who knows what people have dumped there? And foxes are wild – what if one of them bit you?"

She never would, Cassie wanted to say, thinking of Frost's amber eyes and the delicate way the cub could nibble a biscuit from her fingers. But she didn't say it. Who would believe her anyway?

Chapter TWO

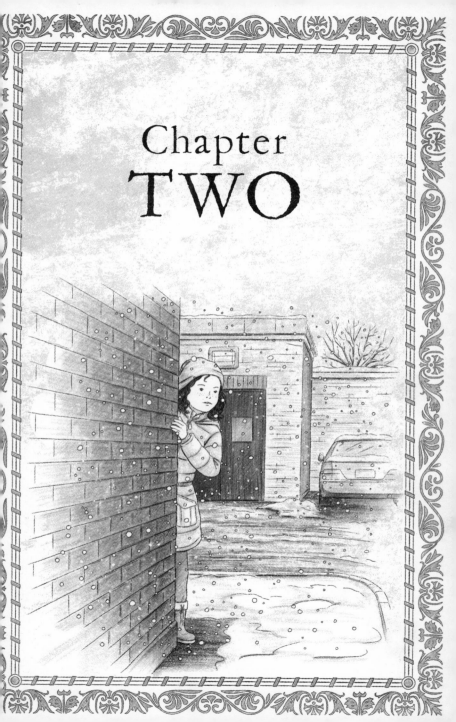

From then on, Cassie's visits to the foxes had to be a lot more secret. Luckily she had William on her side – he didn't want their mum and dad to know about playing football on the waste ground either, so he wouldn't tell. But she had to keep a close eye out for Mrs Morris.

Cassie was pretty sure that if the old lady saw her feeding the foxes again, she would tell her parents. Or worse, the old lady might call the council and ask them to do something about the foxes. Cassie wasn't sure what they could do, but still. She had to be sneaky and her visits had to be short. She made sure to look out for their neighbour whenever she went to the waste ground. She'd worked out that Mrs Morris's kitchen window was in just the right place for the old lady to see her.

Cassie couldn't stop, though. She didn't want to let the foxes go hungry, especially Frost. It was getting colder and colder, and halfway through December there were even a couple of falls of snow. Not quite enough for a proper snowman, but enough for Cassie to put a handful down the back of William's coat after he threw a snowball in her face on the way home from school. It hadn't snowed at all the year before, or the year before that, and Cassie loved it. The snow had come at just the right time too – the last day of school before the holidays and only a few days before Christmas.

"It's so Christmassy," she said to Frost as she fed her some cubes of cheese. There were snowflakes on the little fox's ears, she noticed, as Frost gulped down her treat. And cheese crumbs on her whiskers, until she did one last careful lick around. "We've been making Christmas decorations at school, and we've put our tree up, but now that it's actually snowed it really feels like Christmas. It's like on a Christmas card."

It was wonderful – except that Cassie couldn't stop worrying about the cubs and how much food there was for them to find now that it was so cold.

Besides, she knew that Mum and Mrs Morris were wrong – the foxes weren't fierce. Or the cubs weren't, anyway. Cassie still rarely saw the cubs' mum and dad, and she wasn't sure she'd be brave enough to go close to them if she did.

"You wouldn't ever bite me, would you?" she murmured, and Frost nudged her impatiently, butting her nose into Cassie's arm. She was dancing about, hoping for more food, and leaving tiny, neat paw prints in the thin crust of snow. The waste ground looked cleaner and tidier than Cassie had ever seen it, the straggly bushes and old tyres all turned to snowy humps and lumps. "At least I don't think you'd bite. I'd probably better hurry up and feed you, anyway. There you go, look." She pulled out what she'd saved from lunch. "Half a tuna wrap. Do foxes like fish? I don't, really, but Mum says fish is good for you. She's always putting it in my packed lunches."

Frost seized the wrap eagerly. She had grown tamer since Cassie first started feeding her, back in the summer. She didn't take the food and hurry off to a safe distance, the way she had before. Now she would gobble down the treats Cassie brought right away and then stare up at her hopefully, asking for more. Sometimes she was sitting waiting for Cassie, peering through the brownish weed stems as if she hoped Cassie would come soon. Cassie knew it was because the cub was hungry, but Frost seemed to like seeing her too. They were almost friends.

"I suppose even tuna wraps and cheese are better than beetles," Cassie said thoughtfully. "And maybe there aren't so many beetles now it's colder? Perhaps beetles don't come out in the snow... No, I haven't got another one," she added as Frost gazed into her eyes. "Just half an apple. I'm sorry. I was hungry at lunch so I had some of it. Here." She handed the apple to Frost and the cub crunched it happily.

Cassie sighed. "I'd better go. It's getting dark and Mum thinks I'm playing in the snow with William. Goodnight, Frost." She shivered as she stood up. "It's so cold now."

Frost sniffed hopefully at Cassie's fingers and then obviously decided that there was no more food coming. Her ears pricked up at a scuffling noise from deeper in among the bushes and she trotted away, the white tip of her tail shining in the gloomy afternoon. The sky was an odd yellowish sort of colour and Cassie wondered if it was going to snow again soon.

She pushed her way back through the dead weed stems and eyed the worn-down path through the waste ground. She had to make sure that no one was around – no one who was going to tell on her to her mum, anyway. Everyone seemed to have been put off by the cold and the fading light, though. The courtyard in front of the doors was empty and there was no one out playing in the snow any more. She'd better hurry – if William had already gone back indoors, Mum would be wondering where she was.

Cassie slipped inside and pressed the lift button, and then sighed. She'd forgotten the lift wasn't working again. They only lived on the first floor, but it was a nightmare getting Lucas's pushchair up and down. She raced up the stairs, wanting to get back before Mum realized how long she'd been gone and how dark it was getting. Then she stopped with a little squeak as she swung round the turn in the staircase and nearly ran into a bag of shopping. Cassie pulled herself up sharply and stared at Mrs Morris, sitting surrounded by carrier bags a few steps above her.

"Oh dear, I'm sorry – it's Cassie, isn't it? You live next door?"

Cassie nodded. She wasn't sure if Mrs Morris was cross with her or not.

"I didn't mean to leave everything all over the stairs. I just needed to sit down for a moment. That dratted lift's broken again, you see, and my leg's playing up. It's so slippery out there, it was hard to walk."

"Um ... shall I help with the shopping?" Cassie asked cautiously.

"That would be very nice," Mrs Morris agreed. "I can get up now, I think." She put her hand on the banister and started to haul herself up. Cassie reached out to support her other arm. She'd never thought how difficult it must be for Mrs Morris when the lifts weren't working.

"Thank you, dear. If you could take that bag down there, I can manage this one."

Cassie picked up the shopping and followed Mrs Morris – very, very slowly – up the stairs.

"You're the child who feeds the foxes, aren't you?" Mrs Morris asked, and Cassie swallowed.

"Yes," she admitted, hoping Mrs Morris wasn't going to ask if she was still feeding them.

"I should have said sorry to you before now," Mrs Morris said, puffing slightly.

"To me?" Cassie asked doubtfully, and the old lady turned to look back down at her.

"Yes. I'm sorry I shouted at you that time. I'd just been down to take some rubbish to the bin room and someone had left the door open again. The foxes had got in, and there were ripped bags and rubbish everywhere. I was trying to pick some of it up but it was so disgusting. And then I saw you…"

Cassie nodded. "I would be cross too."

"Ah well." She sighed. "I suppose you're excited about the snow, aren't you?

Snowmen and snowball fights."

"There isn't enough for a snowman, not yet. Maybe tomorrow?"

"Yes…" The old lady shivered. "It's certainly cold enough. I'm sure it's going to snow again." She smiled at Cassie. "You never know, maybe the river will freeze over and you can go skating."

Cassie laughed. She couldn't imagine the river freezing. Their flats were only a few streets away from the Thames, and Mum and Dad often took her and the boys to walk along the side of the river and watch the boats. They had even been down the river on a big trip boat once. The Thames was huge – a great brownish-grey ribbon cutting through the city, glittering on sunny days, deep and dark in the winter. It couldn't ever freeze, it would be like turning some strange beast to ice.

Mrs Morris looked back at Cassie as she unlocked her front door, her head on one side. "I was joking about the skating but the river has frozen over before, you know."

"Really?" Cassie stared at her.

"Oh yes. Not for a few hundred years, mind. But it used to freeze over quite often."

"Did it freeze solid enough to skate on, then?"

Mrs Morris laughed. "Not just skating! They had Frost Fairs. Like a Christmas market, but out on the frozen river."

"You're making that up..." Cassie said doubtfully.

"Not at all, I promise. Here, dear, pass me that bag."

Cassie looked at the old lady and shook her head. Mrs Morris was still quite pale and she looked tired. "I can bring it in, if you want."

"That would be nice." Mrs Morris smiled at her gratefully. "Through here, look."

Cassie couldn't help peering around as they went through the flat to the kitchen. The rooms were just the same shape as her flat next door, but there was only one comfy armchair in the living room and there were bookshelves lining all the walls. It was so tidy too. "Shall I put it here on the counter?"

"That's right. I've got some squash, I'll get you a glass. And a biscuit. To say thank you for helping."

Cassie nodded. Mum wouldn't mind.

She knew Mrs Morris, it wasn't like Cassie was taking food from a stranger. Mrs Morris had to search for the squash – it was at the back of a cupboard and it looked sticky and a bit dusty.

"I got this for when my little great-nieces came to visit," Mrs Morris said, looking at it rather worriedly.

"Orange squash is my favourite," Cassie said, trying to be polite and wondering how long it was since the girls had come. She'd never noticed anyone visiting their neighbour. At least the biscuits looked quite new. "Did you really mean it about the fair?"

"Oh yes. This was hundreds of years ago, though. Back in the 1600s they started having them, I think. There was a different London Bridge then, you see, with big stone columns holding it up. Then they rebuilt the bridge with smaller pillars and it made the water flow faster, so the river doesn't freeze these days."

Cassie sighed. She would have loved to see the river frozen over, although she couldn't imagine a fair on it. "What sort of fair was it?" she asked, taking a cautious sip of squash. It tasted fine. "I mean, they didn't have dodgems and things then, did they?"

"No, no, nothing like that." Mrs Morris looked thoughtful. "But I suppose there would have been sideshows, like the ones we'd see today. Perhaps not coconut shies, because I don't think anyone would have brought coconuts here yet? They'd only just got as far the Americas by then…" Mrs Morris noticed that Cassie was frowning uncertainly at her and shook her head. "I imagine they had a ring toss or that trick where you have to find the ball under a cup."

"I wanted to do that once but my dad said no because it's a con," Cassie pointed out.

Mrs Morris laughed. "I bet it was a con four hundred years ago as well. They had puppet shows, I know that, and even wild-beast shows. In fact, I'm sure I remember reading that Chipperfield's Circus first started back then, with a wild-beast show on the ice. I expect the beast owners didn't treat them very well, though. This is a long time ago, when people thought it was funny to have fights between dogs and bears, and that sort of thing."

"That's horrible."

"Yes... But back then, people thought differently about animals. Hunting was still something that lots of people did every day for food. Even in London, richer people might come out of the city to hunt for sport. Probably not much further out than here, actually."

Cassie frowned. "You couldn't hunt anything round here! Maybe pigeons..."

"But there were hardly any houses here back then!" Mrs Morris looked out of the window at the blocks of flats rising beyond the patch of waste ground. "London was so much smaller. There were Roman walls all round the main part of the city and Southwark was a separate village on the other side of the river."

Cassie stared at her. Southwark was where they were now and it was definitely part of London, even if it was south of the river.

"The only way across was by London Bridge or by boat, so it was almost countryside here. There were buildings along the edge of the river and down the road that led from the bridge but the rest of the area would have been woods and fields."

Cassie smiled, thinking of her foxes. They would probably have liked old

Southwark a lot more. Although there wouldn't have been such good pickings from the bins.

Mrs Morris had been unpacking her shopping bags as she talked and now she took a sausage roll out of one of the packets. She wrapped it in a bit of cling film and handed it to Cassie. "There. You give that to your foxes."

Cassie blinked. How had the old lady known what she had been thinking?

"Like I said, I shouldn't have been so cross that day. I feel sorry for the poor things, always hungry. Especially in weather like this, they must be so cold. I won't tell your mother, Cassie. Now, hadn't you better get back?"

Chapter
THREE

Cassie told her mum about helping Mrs Morris, but she hid the sausage roll in her bottom drawer, under her socks. There was no way she could slip out again that evening – perhaps she'd be able to find an excuse to take it to Frost tomorrow.

As she was getting ready for bed – tiptoeing about, like she always did, so as not to wake up Lucas in his cot in the corner – Cassie stopped to look out of the window at the snow. It had started again while they were eating tea – thick, slow flakes that just kept on coming.

It made Cassie feel sleepy, watching the steady fall. The scruffy, mud-patched grass outside was now completely white again, all the footprints gone. Cassie chewed her bottom lip – the snow was beautiful but all she could think about was the foxes. They must be huddled in their den under the bramble bushes. Or perhaps they were already out looking for food? She shivered, thinking how cold and wet they must be. The wind had picked up a little and the snow was falling faster now, driving almost sideways past the streetlamps.

Then Cassie rubbed fiercely at the glass, which had misted with her breath. Something had moved, out there in the whiteness. A little dark shape that was coming closer towards her.

It looked like Frost – it was hard to tell, it could be one of the other cubs, but Cassie was almost sure. She was padding forward, head down against the wind, her paws leaving deep tracks in the snow – tracks that started to fill up as soon as she had passed.

As Cassie watched, the little fox looked up at the building for a moment and Cassie thought that she saw her. The cub stared back, holding Cassie's gaze. Then she turned to trek on round the side of the flats, perhaps to go and see if there were any pickings in the bin room.

Cassie wriggled out from behind the curtains, letting them fall back against the window with a soft slap. She looked quickly at Lucas, but the noise hadn't disturbed him. He was still fast asleep. William had gone over to their cousin Riley's house after tea for a sleepover. Cassie frowned out at the snow. She'd had a fight with Mum about that at tea – why was William allowed to go for a sleepover and she wasn't? She wasn't that much younger than he was and she could have stayed in her cousin Jessie's room. Will hadn't stuck up for her either. She shook her head crossly. It wasn't important now. Dad was out at work and – yes, she could hear the water running – Mum was about to get in the bath. So maybe, if she was quick, she could slip out after all. She could take that sausage roll to Frost now and no one would ever know she'd been gone.

Cassie crept out into the hallway, lit scarlet and blue and gold by the sparkling lights on the Christmas tree, and grabbed her coat and wellies. She only had her onesie on but it was quite warm and thick, and it wasn't as if she'd be out for long. She took the spare key from the little bowl on the shelf and then slipped out, closing the door behind her as quietly as she could. She just had to hope that Mum didn't go to check on Lucas before getting in the bath, that was all.

She hurried down the stairs and through the front door, watching out for any of their neighbours who might ask her what she was doing out on her own this late. But no one seemed to be about. Cassie crunched through the snow round the side of the block, back to where she'd last seen Frost.

There were tiny paw prints in the snow – just little dips now, almost filled in, but they were deep enough to follow. Frost had clearly gone to look at the bin room, but it was all locked up, and then she'd made her way back to the little playground. There was a litter bin there that was usually full – Cassie wasn't surprised that it was tempting to a hungry fox. As she came closer a little face peered out at her around the slide and she stopped, crouching down.

"I got you something!" she called quietly, undoing the cling film. "Look – a sausage roll – and it's a big one. Mrs Morris gave it to me."

Frost looked around cautiously and then pattered across the snow. She was so light compared to Cassie, if she moved fast her paws hardly sank in at all.

Cassie broke off a piece of sausage roll and held it out to Frost. The fox cub leaned in and gently took it from her fingers, gulping down the treat and then running her tongue around her muzzle eagerly as if she didn't want to miss any crumbs.

"Was that good?" Cassie giggled. "Here you go, have another bit."

She fed the whole sausage roll to the little fox and by the last bit, the cub was leaning up against her knees. Cassie thought she might even be dribbling. "You really liked that, didn't you?" she murmured. "I wish I had some more for you, but that was it. Maybe I could use some of my pocket money to buy you some more? I could ask Mrs Morris to get them for me the next time she goes to the shops. She did say she felt sorry for you all, out here in the snow." Cassie shivered. The snow was still falling – it had settled on her coat and the legs of her onesie felt soggy.

Frost stood up, shook her ears and gave a little yawn. She looked so much happier than she had a few minutes before, when Cassie had seen her from the window. Even her coat seemed brighter and glossier, and her tail was thick and bushy. The food had clearly made her feel lots better. She trotted a few steps away, and then stopped and looked back at Cassie. Her ears were pricked and she had a questioning sort of look. As if she was asking Cassie why she wasn't coming too.

"I've got to go back…" Cassie started to say. "Mum thinks I'm in bed."

Frost put her head on one side and Cassie smiled. "Oh, all right then. Not for long though, OK? I'll be in big trouble if Mum goes to check on Lucas and I'm not there."

She followed the little fox through the snow, still shivering a little. Her wellies were waterproof, but they weren't very warm and she couldn't actually feel her toes any more.

"Where are we going?" she whispered to Frost as they slipped out of the estate and on to the main road. It was oddly quiet tonight. The snow seemed to have muffled all sound – there was nothing but a faint rumble of cars. No one else was out in the frozen night and the road was empty. There weren't even car tracks spoiling the whiteness of the snow and all the parked cars had turned to strange, smooth humps.

"I hope Dad can get back," Cassie muttered. Her dad worked at a print shop, a cycle ride away on the other side of the river. "It's not that far. I guess he'll probably walk home and leave the bike at work."

Frost looked round as she spoke but kept on walking and Cassie kept on following, peering thoughtfully at the streets around her. She needed to remember which way they were going. She wasn't sure that Frost would bring her back home and although they hadn't gone far, everything looked so different in the snow.

Really different. Cassie blinked. She

didn't remember this road at all. She'd thought they were about to turn into the road where her school was, but now they were somewhere else entirely. She looked worriedly back at Frost – but the fox cub had disappeared. Cassie caught her breath in a frightened gasp. Where had Frost gone? She whirled round to look behind her and then yelped in shock as she went skidding in the snow.

"Careful, there..." Someone laughed and set her back on her feet. "Steady now, Cassie. You nearly fell. What were you trying to look at? Those apprentice boys throwing snowballs again, were they?"

Cassie swallowed hard, and stared up at the man smiling down at her and holding her hand. She knew him – but she didn't know how... There was something oddly familiar about the woman and the tall boy standing beside him too. She nodded. She wasn't quite sure what else to do.

The dark street was entirely unfamiliar now – narrow and crowded with houses that seemed to lean over above her, their upper floors sticking out so that they almost touched each other. There were no street lights, just lanterns hung outside houses here and there, and even with the

snow she could see that there was a muddy, dirty gutter down the middle of the road.

Her clothes had changed too – her onesie was gone and now she had on a thick dress, worn over what felt like layers of petticoats, and a warm brown cloak over the top. And her wellies were heavy leather shoes with wooden soles.

"Wool-gathering, sweetheart?" the man asked her, still smiling.

Cassie blinked at him. What did wool-gathering mean?

"Perhaps it's too late for you to be out of bed? Shall I take only Will to the Frost Fair and send you back to stay at home with Lucas and the maid?"

The Frost Fair! The fair on ice that Mrs Morris had told her about! Everything seemed to blur inside Cassie's head, so that she only knew she didn't want to be left behind, like she always was when fun things happened.

"No!" Cassie squeaked indignantly. She was going to the Frost Fair, just like her big brother, and she wouldn't be left at home like baby Lucas.

Will was already getting ahead of them. She pulled hard on her father's hand, and said, "Let's hurry!"

"Perhaps it is a little late?" her mother said, eyeing Cassie worriedly from under the thick woollen hood of her cloak. "It could be rough too, Christopher. All the apprentice boys will be out, racing about the stalls. There'll be such crowds..."

"We'll be careful," Cassie's father promised. "Remember, I've been there printing name cards each night so far and there hasn't been trouble. It's a wonderful sight, Sarah, all those torches burning and everything glittering on the ice. Some were even lighting bonfires on it last night."

"Doesn't that melt through the ice?" Will asked, frowning.

"A little, but the ice is thick enough that it doesn't matter," their father explained. "We had to make sure it was good and solid before we took the printing press out on to the river – I think it must be at least a foot thick."

"Will you print me a card with my name?" Cassie asked pleadingly. "Will you, Father?"

Her father laughed. "I can print your name whenever you like, Cassie!"

"I know but it wouldn't be the same. I want a card that says it was printed on the Thames. I'll keep it forever, I promise."

"Me too," Will added hopefully.

"Well, I'll see, if the booth isn't too busy," their father said, smiling to himself. He had done excellent business over the last two days printing keepsakes from the Frost Fair. Cassie had overheard him promising her mother that she should have a new dress if the sales kept going so well.

"Do you remember the last time the river froze?" her mother asked, and Cassie blinked, trying to look back in time. It was so hard…

"No…?" she whispered uncertainly.

"She's too young!" Will said, laughing. "*I* remember."

"I do too!" Cassie protested, even though she didn't at all.

"We took you to walk on the ice," her mother told her, smiling. "You were only tiny, Cassie, I'm not surprised you don't remember."

"I'll remember this Frost Fair forever," Cassie said determinedly.

"We're nearly there," her father promised, feeling her tug on his hand. "Very close – look, do you see, between the houses?"

Cassie peered forward and saw a mass of golden lights bobbing in the darkness – the fair, stretched out across the frozen river.

Chapter
FOUR

Cassie had seen the river many times before. It was often busy – thronged with small rowing boats ferrying passengers from one bank to the other, or travelling up and down – but she had never seen it like this. A huge crowd swirled about on the ice, talking and laughing and pointing at the sights to be seen.

Most people were in plain clothes, with warm cloaks and had wooden pattens tied over their shoes to protect against the chill of the ice. Several beggars in ragged clothes were asking for coins. But here and there the light from the lanterns and flaring torches shone on gold-braided coats and silken dresses under fur. The richer people of London, perhaps even courtiers from the king's palace, were out to see the magic of the frozen city for themselves.

"Keep close," Cassie's mother warned her. "There's such a crowd, it would be easy to lose you. What shall we do first, then?" she added, smiling at Cassie's excited face, the way she kept turning round to look at all the different stalls and sideshows. "Would you like to see a puppet show?"

"They're playing at ninepins over there!" Will said excitedly, pointing ahead. "And look, a bear!"

Cassie shuddered. The bear was caged up next to a fenced-off ring. They were going to make it fight later, she supposed. She had never been to see the bears at the Bear Garden out in Southwark, since it wasn't a fit place to take a child, her mother always said. But she had heard her father's apprentices at the printers talking about bear-baiting and she thought it sounded desperately cruel.

"Perhaps we should buy some gingerbread as a treat," her mother said gently, noticing her worried look. "Look, there's a stall just there, close to your father's printing booth. We'll buy some, and then you can eat it while you watch the puppets."

Cassie nodded. She loved gingerbread and they hardly ever had it. She could smell the spices from here. As they waited their turn at the stall, Cassie gazed around at the different sideshows and then she clutched at Will's arm. "Look! A boat on wheels!"

"Don't be silly," her brother started to say, then he stopped. "Oh."

Cassie gave him a triumphant look

and then went back to watching the boat being drawn past. It was a small sailing boat, but it was being hauled over the ice by a team of men pulling on ropes. The sails were just flapping a little in the wind and it was laden with a crowd of people, laughing and waving as they slid past.

"Here." Her mother put a piece of gingerbread into Cassie's mittened hands, and Cassie breathed a dark, exciting sniff of it. It smelled exotically warm, the perfect thing to eat out on the frozen river. She nibbled the edge cautiously, and felt the heat of the ginger and cinnamon fill her mouth.

"Cassie! Will! This way! Come and print your names." Cassie's father waved at them from beside the printing press, and Cassie and Will hurried over to stand beside the huge machine. Cassie couldn't help looking worriedly at the ice underneath it, but there were no cracks. She watched Benjamin, her father's apprentice, fit the metal type into the frame. Most of the message was already there – he just had to add the letters for her name and then Will's, further down.

"There." He smiled at Cassie. "You want to pull the devil's tail?"

Cassie nodded excitedly. She had visited the printworks often, but she was hardly ever allowed to touch the great presses. Her father lifted her up to reach the great metal handle that pulled the weight of

the press down on to the type, pressing it down hard into the paper. Then Benjamin rolled the frame out of the press and opened it up, lifting out the sheet of paper and trimming it deftly into smaller cards. He presented them to Will and Cassie with a flourish.

Cassie stroked the thick linen-rich paper admiringly and smiled at the pretty edging around the card. Her name looked so elegant in the smart black lettering. *Cassandra Daunt.*

"It's beautiful," she told her father and Benjamin.

"Be careful – the ink needs a while to dry," her father pointed out. "Sixpence please, young lady." Then he laughed at Cassie's horrified face. "I'm teasing you, sweetheart. Here, that should be dry now. Tuck it away in your pocket and run and see the puppet show."

Cassie nodded, her cheeks scarlet – Benjamin was smirking at her and Will rolling his eyes. She put the card away carefully in the little leather pocket hanging at the waist of her dress and turned to look at the crowd around the puppet booth, so that no one would see the tears smarting in her eyes. Why did everyone always have to make fun of her?

She sniffed crossly and muttered something about going to watch the puppets to her mother.

"Come back here to the printing booth straight after!" her mother called to her, and Cassie waved to show she'd heard. She walked around the edge of the crowd at the puppet show, wondering how she could get to the front to see what was happening. If she went back and asked, her father or maybe even Benjamin would lift her up on to their shoulders, but she didn't want to. She was still annoyed with them for laughing and she didn't want to sound like a little girl begging for favours.

In the end she spotted a gap in the crowd and went for it, burrowing forward like a mole. Most people let her creep past, though a few did complain that she should wait her turn.

"Let the little one through," one old woman told a couple of larger boys in front of her, and Cassie thanked her politely. At last she was almost at the front and able to see the stage set up on the bed of a wagon, the puppets dancing in front of a dark curtain.

It was the tale of St George and the dragon, with the dragon a great green beast, dangling from several strings so that he could coil and leap around the mailed knight. Cassie squeaked delightedly as the creature seemed to breathe a plume of fire, though she wondered afterwards if perhaps it had only been a puff of silken fabric. It had happened so quickly and cleverly that it was hard to tell.

St George swung his sword, and the dragon collapsed to the floor of the stage, groaning sadly and then turning his paws upwards in a deathlike pose. The crowd cheered enthusiastically and then started to melt away before the puppeteers could close the curtain and hurry out to pass around a hat for coins.

Cassie stayed watching, hoping that wasn't the end and there would be more, but then a young boy in a dark coat came out and held a hat meaningfully under her nose. Reluctantly, she gave him the penny her mother had put into her pocket. She supposed he was one of the puppeteers, perhaps the one who had made the dragon dance about so wildly, and she longed to ask him about it. But he moved on, hurrying after the other people in the crowd and sweet-talking them for pennies.

Cassie was about to go back to the printer's booth when a flash of reddish-brown caught her eye, somewhere around the puppeteers' wagon. At first Cassie thought that it was one of the puppets – maybe it had fallen down below the curtain. She crouched down to look better and saw a sharp, pointed face peering back at her.

Cassie laughed out loud at the strange little thing gazing at her hungrily with golden-brown eyes. And then suddenly, a strange wave of homesickness rolled over her, as if the ice had melted and the river was sucking her under. Cassie leaned against the wagon wheel, gasping for breath.

Frost!

She didn't belong here. Cassie looked around wildly, trying to balance the two lives that both seemed to be in her head at once. She was Cassie, daughter of Christopher Daunt the printer, out exploring the Frost Fair – and she was Cassie, a girl out on a snowy night, following the fox cub she'd been feeding since the summer holidays.

"Which am I?" she whispered to the

little fox – the only part that seemed to belong to both Cassies. But the fox was gone. The puppet-show boy had come stomping back over, grumbling because there was hardly any money in his hat. He had frightened the fox away and now he growled at Cassie.

"Show's over. Get gone," he muttered as he tramped past her and round to the end of the wagon. But Cassie was still too confused to move. She stayed leaning by the wheel, blinking to herself and wondering what to do. Where to go? What had happened to the little fox? There were angry voices behind her and she listened without really meaning to, too bewildered to move away.

"Is that all you got?" a voice said irritably.

"I did my best!" the boy snapped. "Can't help it if half the crowd left before I got out there! We need another boy to pass around the hat – I can't do everything."

"*Another* boy?" The puppeteer laughed. "I can't even afford to keep *you* on takings like this!"

"You said I could have some money for a pie when we got to the fair," the boy moaned. "I'm hungry. I haven't had anything to eat."

"A pie? There was bread and cheese aplenty, boy. I'm not giving you money to go off gallivanting, not after yesterday."

There was a grumpy silence and then the boy said sulkily, "There wasn't any bread and cheese left, you ate it all. And I wasn't gone that long."

"All afternoon," his master hissed.

"Half a dozen shows we could have done! It's good takings at the *The Dog and Duck*, always. I needed you there and you were off watching the duck-baiting with those tearaway lads. So don't you go begging me for a pie now, you lazy lump! And don't you tell me *I* ate the bread and cheese, I haven't had a crumb. I've been too busy chasing after you!"

The two lives swirled inside Cassie's head, making her feel dizzy. *The Dog and Duck* was a pub close to their flat, where her dad liked to go to watch the football with Grandpa sometimes. *And* it was a pub over the river that she'd heard her father talk about, in St George's Fields. His apprentices had gone over there to watch dogs being set on the ducks. St George's Fields was a swampy, marshy sort of place, where there were ducks aplenty. Much of the land south of the river was like that, Cassie thought vaguely. Her father's apprentices had been late back too and he'd been angry. But her mother had persuaded him not to dock their wages, reminding him that they were young and they'd learn...

Cassie squeaked as the pointed foxy face popped up again, looking at her from under a booth advertising a magical phoenix bird, the only one in captivity. She darted after it, sure that somehow Frost would show her the way home. After all, it was following the fox cub that had brought her here, wasn't it? Cassie squeezed her hands into fists inside her mittens. She didn't understand what was happening. No one had brought her here.

She *lived* here. But at the same time…

The fox, Cassie told herself. *There's something special about her, I know there is. I know I've seen her before – but then I'm sure I never have… I've got to follow the fox. Then perhaps I'll find out what's happening.* She cast one last worried look back across the ice and the crowd at the printing booth. Then she drew her brown cloak tight around her and darted after the little red-brown shape.

The fox stayed hidden, creeping between the booths so cleverly that Cassie was almost sure the creature had shown herself on purpose at the puppet show. She was never visible for more than a moment now, just peeping round every so often to see that Cassie was still following.

Cassie stumbled along on the rough ice,

made slippery by so many passing feet, panting a little. Even on the ice she was getting hot under her thick cloak, but she couldn't slow down – she mustn't get left behind.

"Cassie!"

She froze for a moment but didn't look back. It was Will's voice – and there was her father calling too. Of course they would chase after her. Her mother had told her to stay close. Cassie hurried, trying to run in her wooden-soled shoes and the fox cub seemed to speed up too, scurrying between the stalls, her white tail tip bobbing.

"Cassie, stop! Come back here!" her father roared, and Cassie turned round anxiously. He was so close! He had almost caught her up. She shook her head worriedly. She should do as she was

told – why on earth was she running off?
She was going to get into trouble, and—

No.

She had to catch the fox. She raced
on faster and saw the fox streaking
away ahead of her.

"Frost!" Cassie cried. Then she felt her ankle turn underneath her and she gasped and slammed down hard on the ice, hitting her head with a frightened cry.

Chapter
FIVE

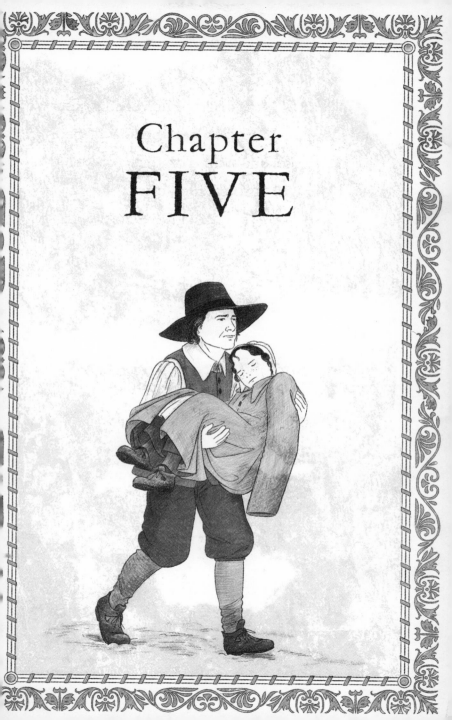

"Cassie! Cassie, wake up! What were you doing?"

"Is she dead?" Will's voice was scared.

"No ... no. She's just stunned. She must have hit her head on the ice when she fell."

Cassie blinked and stared up at her father's worried, angry face.

"There! You see – she's awake now." He sounded as though he hadn't been completely sure she was going to wake up. Looking at him, Cassie thought that might be what was making him so cross.

"Why were you running away from us?" her father demanded. "You could hear us calling, couldn't you? Why didn't you come straight back to the booth like you were told?"

"My head hurts," Cassie whispered. It was easier than trying to answer all those questions, especially when she didn't *know* the answers. Why had she been running? She knew it was important to go straight back to her mother. What on earth had she been doing?

Her father huffed, his breath steaming in the cold, and scooped her up in his arms. Cassie huddled into his coat, her eyes half closed. She was starting to feel better but she still didn't understand why she had been running away.

As they passed the puppet booth, the memory of a little furry face made her gasp with surprise and her father looked down at her. "Oh, so you're awake again? Good. You can make your excuses to your mother – she was frantic. What happened, Cassie? Why did you run off?"

"There was a fox," Cassie murmured,

trying to remember. It didn't really make sense to her either and she had a feeling that her father wasn't going to understand.

"A fox," he said blankly. "In the city? No, child."

"There was," Cassie insisted as her mother came rushing up to kiss her and cry and tell her off, all at once.

"She says she saw a fox," her father explained.

"But ... there aren't any foxes here." Cassie's mother shook her head. "And if there were, even a fox is no excuse for disappearing like that! You had me worried to death!"

"I did see one." Cassie wriggled out of her father's arms and slipped down to stand on the ice. "I know I did."

"Cassie, foxes are country beasts," her
father explained. "They don't come into
London."

"Perhaps she's still dazed," Cassie's
mother said worriedly. "She's imagining
things. I'd better take her home."

"Oh, no! No!" Cassie pleaded. "You said we could see the dancing and visit the booths…"

"*You* said you would be good and stay close," her mother snapped, and Cassie looked down at her feet miserably. Her mother was right. Whatever had she been thinking?

Cassie rolled over in bed then froze, listening. Had her mother heard her stir? She had been up and down the stairs all evening, looking in to the bedroom where Cassie was asleep on a small truckle bed next to the big four-poster. Lucas was asleep in his wooden cradle at the end of the bed too. It seemed as if he or Cassie only had to twitch and their mother was there, fussing.

But there was no sound from below now, no creaking on the stairs. Cassie sighed. She wasn't tired, especially not when she knew that Will was still out enjoying all the sights of the Frost Fair. She had ruined her special treat and all because of a fox – a fox that her mother and father were certain she couldn't even have seen.

A sound from outside in the street made her roll over again and then scramble up on to her knees so that she could look out of the window behind her. She pulled the blankets up around her neck like a cloak and peered out into the street. The moon was shining on to the snow, leaving it glowing blue-white. In the street outside the window sat a small dark shape, with pricked ears and a thick white-tipped tail.

Cassie pressed her fingers against the tiny panes of glass, flinching at the cold. There was definitely a fox out there. She had never seen a real fox before today but she had seen pictures in a book of her mother's, *Aesop's Fables*, and she wasn't imagining it. She hadn't imagined it earlier that night either.

The fox seemed to see her looking. She stood up and moved so that she was under her window, but a little further out into the street. Then it barked at her – that was the sound she had heard before, Cassie realized.

It was almost as if the fox was calling.

Cassie stared down at it doubtfully and then scrambled out of bed. She would show her mother! Then perhaps

everyone would stop being so cross.
Perhaps they would even let her go back
to the fair? Feeling hopeful, she dragged
on her petticoats and stockings, and then
her warm woollen dress. Then she took
one last look out of the window before
hurrying downstairs. The fox was still
there, looking up at her.

Cassie was expecting to find her mother in the kitchen. Once they'd come back home she had given the maid, Margery, the evening off to go to the fair, so Mother would be preparing supper for Cassie's father and Will herself. But the kitchen was empty, the fire just a few embers and no lamps were lit.

Cassie whisked back to peer into the parlour and saw that her mother was by the fire – asleep, with a piece of embroidery sliding off her lap. Cassie hesitated in the doorway. She ought to wake her mother and show her the fox, that was why she'd come downstairs. But what if Mother woke up in a bad temper? She did sometimes, especially if she hadn't meant to fall asleep.

"Mother?" Cassie whispered, but her

mother didn't stir. Cassie tiptoed past her to look out of the parlour window on to the street. The fox gazed back at her and, from this close, Cassie could see the pleading look in her golden-brown eyes. She made that strange barking cry again and Cassie bit her lip, wondering what the creature wanted.

"You got me into trouble before," she murmured and then she sighed. The fox looked so cold out there in the snow, even with her thick fur. What was she doing here in the city? Her parents had been so certain that foxes didn't belong here. "You should go back home," Cassie whispered through the glass. "If you stay, someone might set a dog on you." Or perhaps someone would turn the poor animal into a pair of fur mittens...

"Shoo!" Cassie hissed as the fox barked again. Someone else was going to hear that soon. She darted back past her mother and went to the front of the house, lifting the latch and peering around the heavy wooden door. The fox pattered over to her through the snow and Cassie stared down at her, surprised. She seemed almost tame. Her ears twitched curiously as she looked back at Cassie.

"You're a pretty little thing." Cassie crouched down, wondering if the fox would snap if she tried to stroke her. "Are you hungry?" she wondered. "Stay there."

She pushed the door almost closed and hurried back to the kitchen, picking up a scrap of cold bacon from the larder and some stale bread. As an afterthought, she took the candle lantern that was hanging on a nail by the door to the yard, lighting it with a taper from the fire. At the door, she pulled on her cloak, putting the hood up around her face. It was so cold outside that she needed to wrap up, even if she was only going out for a few minutes.

The fox gulped down the scraps hungrily as Cassie tore the bread and bacon into tiny pieces to feed her, but she was careful not to nip Cassie's fingers.

When all the food was gone, she sniffed at Cassie and then licked her hand as if she was grateful.

"You should go home," Cassie told the fox again. "Go home, girl." But the fox just laid her muzzle on Cassie's knee and looked up at her, eyes still hopeful.

"I can't get any more food," Cassie told her, cautiously stroking the top of her head. "Not without it being noticed. Mother might think Margery or Benjamin took it – they'll get into trouble. And if I stay out here much longer, someone will see."

The fox heaved a sigh and turned away, trotting out to the middle of the street. Then she stopped and looked back over her shoulder at Cassie standing in the doorway. She seemed surprised, as though she had expected Cassie to follow her.

"I can't come with you," Cassie said, but deep inside she felt that same strange longing. Out on the icy river, she had seen the fox and known that she had to go with her. It was important, somehow. The little fox needed her – and she needed the fox.

Cassie swallowed and looked back into the house. Her mother was still in the parlour, asleep. No one would know she had gone. And she'd be back soon, wouldn't she?

Cassie picked up the lantern and drew the door closed behind her with a quiet click of the latch. Then she followed the fox cub out into the snow.

Chapter
SIX

The fox set off quickly, padding along the snowy street with her paws lifted high and her ears flattened against the cold wind. Cassie thought that it was probably going to snow again soon. The night seemed to have turned even colder and heavy clouds were starting to cover the sky. They were blocking the moonlight and Cassie was very glad she had brought the lantern.

"Where are we going?" she called to the little fox, a few minutes later as they passed the great church of St Dunstan's. Cassie stopped for a moment to catch her breath and to look up at the two painted wooden giants who struck their bells to tell the quarter hours on the church clock, as she always did. It was late – nine o'clock already. How much longer would the crowds stay at the Frost Fair, with the weather worsening? The streets seemed almost empty now but she suspected that soon they would be full of chilled merrymakers on their way home from the fair.

Cassie called again. "Are you going home?"

The fox looked back at her, her pink tongue showing as she panted a little, but she didn't answer. Cassie hadn't really expected her to, of course, but there was something about her, something that seemed strange and special. It didn't seem impossible that she would talk.

Cassie wondered how far they were going – where the fox's home was. If her mother and father were right – that foxes didn't live in the city – the fox's den must be quite a long way away. What if her mother woke and found her gone? She glanced over her shoulder anxiously. They'd already come a good distance from her home.

Cassie stood wavering in the snow, uncertain what to do. The fox looked back and saw her standing there, and made a worried little yipping noise. She came padding through the snow to Cassie and stared up at her pleadingly, her eyes shining just a little in the light of the lantern. *Help me*, she seemed to say, and Cassie nodded.

She pushed all thoughts of home and her mother and the trouble she would be in firmly away, and began to walk again. It was an effort, though. She wasn't used to walking in the soft snow, it seemed to make her legs work differently. They hadn't even started to climb Ludgate Hill and her legs were aching already. But she went a little faster as they came in sight of the cathedral. It seemed to change every time she saw it, the walls a little higher each day.

Her father loved to take her and Will to look at it. He had made Cassie shiver, describing the way the fire had taken hold of the old church of St Paul's and the rats had come streaking away in a great tide of dirty fur, shrieking and scrambling in panic past the watching crowd. Then after them had crept a slow tide of shining metal, the lead from the cathedral roof, melted by the heat.

Her father had been an apprentice himself then, seventeen years before.

His master's printworks had been swallowed up by the Great Fire. They had carried away the cases of type, he told Cassie and Will, and as much of the presses as they could, but the fire had been too fast, too hungry. There had been hard years afterwards, camped out in the ruins of the building, trying to raise the money to repair and rebuild the house and the workshop, and keep their livelihood going.

It was difficult to tell now where the fire had raced through the city, except for the neat, sturdy brick houses that had been built in the ruined streets. But it would be a long time before the new cathedral was finished. Years and years, Cassie reckoned. It was so big and so grand, it was bound to take forever.

"Are you stopping to look too?"

Cassie murmured to the little fox as they hesitated at Ludgate itself. Cassie never liked the gate. It always seemed to her that the poor men in the prison up above were watching her as she passed through and the fox cub seemed to have the same eerie feeling. They slunk under the stone gate together and hurried on to get a better view of the cathedral.

But outside the churchyard, the fox stopped altogether, pacing around in a small circle and sniffing anxiously at the snow. She seemed to be dithering, looking first one way and then the other.

"Towards the river?" Cassie suggested, but the fox only looked up at her uncertainly, and paced a little way towards Watling Street and then back again.

"Are you lost?" Cassie asked, crouching down and shivering as the hem of her cloak trailed in the snow. "I can't help! I don't even know where you're trying to go. Where you're taking me..." She looked around worriedly. It had seemed to make sense, following the fox when the little creature knew where she was going. A lost fox was a different matter entirely.

Cassie frowned. "Unless I'm meant to

help you get to wherever it is you're trying to go," she muttered. "Maybe that's why it felt so important that I came." She stood up again, gazing around. "I don't think we should stay here too long. There are guards around the cathedral, protecting the building site. I should think they'll chase us away. Besides, it's so dark now. People will see our lantern and that might not be good."

Her mother was always warning her to stay close to home when she went to meet the other children from the street and she was hardly ever allowed to go out in the dark. To hear Cassie's mother tell it, London was a den of thieves. But then she had come from the country and still found the city a strange and daunting place sometimes.

A shadow flitted across the street in front of them and Cassie swallowed and tucked the lantern underneath her cloak. "It isn't as if I've got anything to steal," she whispered to herself. "I don't think a thief would bother robbing a child…"

She huddled the hood of her cloak closer around her face, feeling the comfort of the warm wool. It would hide the pale smudge of her face too, she thought, her heart beating a little faster. She didn't like her brown cloak much, but it was dark. All the better to melt away into the shadows. "Over here," she whispered to the fox, pressing closer to the wall. "We need to stay out of sight."

But the little fox wasn't listening to her. She was standing out in the middle of the street, ears pricked and one paw lifted.

She looked alert, worried.

"What is it? Have you worked out where we're going?"

Then the fox's ears flattened back and she shrieked in panic as the strange shadow they had seen before came surging back towards her. Not a pickpocket, as Cassie had feared, but a dog. A skinny, sharp-toothed stray, looking for a fight.

The little fox darted about, trying to dodge the bigger creature's jaws. She was whining with fright and Cassie gasped as the dog snapped horribly close to the fox cub's shoulder. "Leave her alone!" she cried out, entirely forgetting to be quiet and stealthy. "Get away! Get away!"

The dog glanced sideways at her and growled but it didn't seem scared of Cassie at all. The fox was panting now, tiring as the great beast chased her here and there in the snow.

"I need a stick," Cassie said to herself, but everything was covered in snow. She couldn't even see a stone to throw.

The fox cub let out a heartbreaking whimper, slipping on to the snow as the dog loomed over her, and Cassie screamed again. She couldn't let this happen. She set down the lantern and dragged off a heavy wooden-soled shoe. Then she flung it at the dog's head. She stood there, with her stockinged foot in the snow, pressing her hands against her mouth. What if the dog turned on her now?

But it didn't. It stood up, shaking its head as though it felt dazed, and growled at Cassie and the fox. Then it sloped away into the darkness.

Cassie picked up her lantern and crouched down by the trembling cub, stroking the red-brown fur and checking for wounds. There was a scratch on the little fox's muzzle but otherwise she seemed unhurt. She crept closer to Cassie, huddling against her skirts and whimpering.

"This isn't the place for you to be," Cassie murmured as the cub shivered next to her. "We have to find where you belong – it isn't safe here. I wish I knew where you came from." She looked at the fox doubtfully. "I suppose the closest bit of wooded country to here is across the river. Did you come that way? Over London Bridge? I don't see why you'd want to come into the city, though I suppose you are quite a curious little thing. It seems a long way to travel, just following your nose."

At this the fox poked her pointed muzzle out of the folds of Cassie's cloak and sniffed the air loudly. Then she let out a whine, a soft, hopeless noise that caught at Cassie's heart. "Don't say that!" she whispered. "We'll find it. Do you really not know the way?"

It seemed clear that the fox didn't. She stared at her paws, her ears drooping.

"No, you don't. Well…" Cassie looked around. "You were on the river, on the ice…" Which meant that the fox hadn't actually needed to cross London Bridge at all, Cassie realized, even if she had come from the south side of the river. She could just have walked down on to the ice, if she found a flattish bit of bank, or one of the flights of steps that led down to the landing stages.

"Do foxes walk down steps? I don't know… Did you follow something? Were you hunting, maybe?" Cassie blinked. "Oh! That boy! The puppeteer's boy… He went off hunting, didn't he? At *The Dog and Duck*, and his master was so angry with him for wasting all of yesterday afternoon… That's where they were, in St George's Fields, where it's all marshy and there are ducks."

She gazed down at the fox. "That sounds very much the sort of place where a fox would live too. And I first saw you by the puppet-show wagon." Cassie pressed her hand over her mouth, laughing. "Did you eat their bread and cheese, little fox? Was that why they both said they hadn't had any?"

The fox looked back at Cassie with her head on one side and then a pinkish tongue shot out and ran around her muzzle, as if she were remembering those cheese crumbs.

"I bet you did…" Cassie held out her hand to the fox cub, then patted her leg. "Come on. This way. I don't know which way you came in the wagon, but I think we can go back across the ice. I'm not sure the guards would let a fox go across London Bridge, or me either. And besides," Cassie shuddered, "I don't like seeing the heads."

The heads of traitors were impaled on spikes at the southern gatehouse of the bridge and they made Cassie feel sick. She always shut her eyes and hung on to her mother's cloak when they went that way to visit her aunt, who lived over the other side of the river on St Margaret's Hill, not far from the bridge. But there was no one for her to hold on to now, so she would have to look.

"We'll go down the steps and on to the ice instead," she explained to the fox as they trotted towards the river. "But we'll have to be careful, in case we meet Father or Will."

That evening, her family had gone down the Temple Stairs to get on to the ice just where the Frost Fair began. But now she and the fox had already walked further on, past the fair towards the bridge.

It should be quieter here, Cassie hoped. There was less chance of someone stopping her and asking where she was off to on her own. She could hear the sounds of the Frost Fair further up the river –

music, shouting and the noise of a lot of people having a good time.

She led the fox down towards the river, past a grand new church with a tower and tall glass windows. Newly built since the fire again, Cassie guessed, looking around to see where they could get down to the river. A dank, rather fishy smell of boats and boathouses led her down another smaller alley, and they saw a set of stone steps leading directly into the ice.

There were two open rowing boats moored there still, sitting sadly in the ice with little ripples frozen around them. It was odd to step down and walk past them – it made Cassie feel as if she was walking out on to the water. She hesitated a little before she put her foot down, as if the ice would melt away and she'd fall into the dark water of the Thames instead.

The fox cub flinched as she stepped out on to the snow-covered river. "It isn't far," Cassie told the fox. "Only as far as it was from St Paul's to here. We'll hurry. And then you'll almost be back home. I don't know exactly where *The Dog and Duck* is, but you'll know where you are, won't you? Once you're back on your side of the river?"

The fox plodded forwards, shivering a little now. It was starting to snow again, those clouds that Cassie had noticed building up even more thickly. Cassie wrapped her cloak tighter around her, trying to ward off the biting wind that seemed to swirl straight down the frozen river. Then the two of them set off across the ice.

Chapter
SEVEN

Chapter
SEVEN

Cassie struggled up the snow-piled stairs, with the little fox waiting for her a few steps above. She seemed much happier now she was back on the south side of the river. Her ears were brightly pricked again and she had a new energy, despite the freezing cold. Cassie smiled as the fox bounded eagerly up the steps, sure that this meant they were going in the right direction.

It seemed even colder on this bank of the river, though. She was regretting that she had not brought an extra muffler or her mother's mittens to wear on top of her own. She didn't think she had ever been so cold and the snow was thickening now, blowing sideways into her face as she reached the top of the stairs. The light of the lantern spread around Cassie in a tiny circle, so that the world seemed only to be a thousand falling snowflakes and no more.

She lifted the lantern up higher, trying to see where they were. She only came to the south bank of the river rarely, when they visited her aunt. But she lived a good way further along from here and Cassie wasn't at all sure where they were. The south bank of the river was well known for its theatres and skittle alleys and the bear pits, but looking around in the snow-filled darkness, Cassie thought it was the loneliest place she had ever seen.

The fox was busily sniffing about in the hedge and Cassie hoped that she was finding the scent of her home. She paced away up the path and then looked back, waiting for Cassie to follow her.

"I hope it isn't far…" Cassie sighed. "My feet have turned to lumps of ice, I can't feel them any more." *And once you've found your home again, I'll have to go all the way back to mine,* she said to herself. *On my own.* That thought made her feel even colder.

She followed the fox down the lane, watching its white tail tip in the faint glow of the lantern. There seemed to be small houses on either side, but there were hardly any lights showing. It was so hard to see anything that Cassie almost screamed when a huge building loomed up ahead of them out of the snow.

"What *is* that?" Cassie yelped, her voice shaking. She'd thought they were heading for open countryside, where the foxes lived, but this building was enormous.

Or at least it had been. As she crept a little closer she saw that it was half ruined, only the tumbledown shell left behind.

It had been grand once though, she thought. A great circular building, with gaping holes in the walls. Cassie went closer, slipping on the snow, and peered in through one of the broken gaps. The building had an open roof and she realized what it was, what it had been. A great theatre, one of the old kind, with the stage in the middle and tiers of seats all around. She stood there, trying to imagine what it had been like, lifting her lantern to see the broken galleries and imagining them full of people.

Then she whirled round, her heart thumping as the fox let out a sharp warning bark. Someone was coming!

Cassie could hear them, talking and laughing as they trudged down the lane, probably making for the very stairs she had come up by. They must have been to one of the newer theatres along the riverbank.

The fox came creeping through the fallen stones to stand right next to her, shivering, and Cassie hid her lantern under her cloak. She didn't want to be seen out here on her own – she could hardly explain that she wasn't alone, she was with a fox cub. Her mother's warnings were in the back of her mind too. These could be thieves, there was no way to tell. Cassie blinked at them through the snowfall, hesitating. Not everyone could be a robber, after all. They might take her home…

Home. Where there was a warm fire

and her mother would surely have missed her by now. Father and Will would be back from the Frost Fair too. Perhaps they had gone out again already, to search for her. Cassie started up, reaching to pull out her lantern, thinking suddenly that if she called to the noisy gang passing by, they would come and fuss over her, perhaps even carry her back across the ice. But then the fox cub whined quietly, and Cassie sank back and petted her ears.

"I didn't mean it," she whispered. "I won't leave you, not till you're safe. Come on," she added as the voices died away down the lane. "Let's go."

They struggled on through the snow but the short rest by the broken old theatre seemed to have made Cassie more tired, not less. It looked like they were walking into a wilder sort of country now. There were no more buildings, just a great long stretch of gleaming whiteness, with a hedge here and there, or a great ditch full of snow. It was hard to make each step when her feet were so numb with cold and several times she stumbled. The fox seemed to see that she was struggling and she came closer to Cassie, nosing gently at her legs and nudging her on.

"I was supposed to be helping you," Cassie whispered. "Not the other way round. Are we nearly there?"

Suddenly, the little fox stood still, her ears twitching and turning, her eyes bright with excitement. She had sensed something, Cassie was sure. Could she smell her home? Her fox family?

Cassie watched as she barked, a funny little yipping bark, a sort of "Wuh-wuh-wuh!" noise. And from across the stretch of snow in front of them, another fox barked back.

Cassie's fox raced away, dashing over the snowy ground and disappearing into the darkness. She was gone so quickly that Cassie didn't even have time to call goodbye. She gulped back the tears that seemed to rise up inside her and pinched the back of her hand crossly. Why was she crying? She had only known the fox for a few hours but it seemed longer. Their journey had felt so important – and now it was over.

Cassie staggered on a few steps, trying to see the foxes, but there was no sign of them at all. The tears on her face felt as though they were freezing on to her skin and she brushed at them fiercely, scrubbing at her cheeks with her mittened hands. She stumbled a little, and then shrieked as the snow beneath her feet seemed to disappear and she went tumbling headlong into a deep pit.

There was snow in her mouth and in her ears and everywhere, and Cassie lay gasping. What had happened? She struggled to sit up and tried to work out where she was. The lantern had gone out in the fall, and all she could see was darkness and a faint patch of lighter sky above.

Now that she was sitting up, the hole didn't seem to be that deep. Cassie guessed that it was just a ditch that had been covered up with snow. Even so, it was too deep for her to climb out of easily with numbed hands and feet. Slowly she got to her feet and pulled off her mittens, wincing as she tried to flex her frozen, stinging fingers. She reached up and tried to grab at the dead grasses that were trailing over the edge of the ditch, hoping to pull herself out. But the grasses were slippery and brittle at the same time, and her fingers just weren't working. The clumps slid out of her hands and she slumped back into the ditch.

"Th-th-this is stupid," Cassie told herself, her teeth chattering. "It isn't deep. I can get out. I can."

But she couldn't.

Cassie wrapped her arms around her knees, hugging herself hard and trying not to cry. She had been scared of the dark and the flurrying snowflakes but that seemed like nothing. Now she was actually, properly frightened. What if she never got out? The snow could keep falling and cover her over. What would her mother and father think? They'd never even know what had happened to her. That seemed almost worse than never going home and Cassie pressed her fist hard into her mouth.

She had to get out!

She struggled up again and yelled, "Help! Please! Help me, I'm stuck!" Then she stopped, listening hopefully, and shivered as a strange echo of her own cry came back. No one else answered her but Cassie shook her head determinedly and called again.

She kept shouting for what felt like hours, until her throat hurt and the cold had stripped away her voice. No one came.

She leaned against the edge of the ditch, sniffling hopelessly, but then she heard the crunching patter of little footsteps, coming closer.

"Is that you?" she whispered hoarsely.

"Little fox?"

There was a scrabbling noise and a shadowy patch of deeper darkness appeared above her. The fox cub whined softly and Cassie made a sort of gasping noise, halfway between a sob and a laugh. "I thought you'd gone. You came back for me." Then she added sadly, "But I don't think you can get me out."

The fox cub seemed to agree. She sniffed all the way along the edge of the ditch, treading carefully so as to avoid sliding in herself, and then whined again. Cassie wasn't sure if she was imagining it, but the whine sounded rather desperate.

Then the fox pattered away and Cassie felt her eyes fill with tears. Being left again felt almost worse than the first time.

Except that the fox cub hadn't left. Cassie could hear paws padding over the snow, more paws this time, and there was yipping and whining too, as if the foxes were talking to each other. Had the little fox brought her brothers and sisters to help?

"What are you doing?" Cassie whispered. Then she squeaked and held up her arm to shield her face as a spray of snow and dirt spattered over her. She stood as far back as she could, blinking bemusedly.

It took her a few minutes to work out their plan and then she began to laugh weakly. They were so clever! They were digging her a path out – a shallow slope to climb up, instead of the steep side of the ditch. The foxes were rescuing her!

It took a good half an hour of digging while Cassie watched, trying to remember to stamp her feet and rub her hands together to keep as warm as she could. But it was hard when she was so tired. All she really wanted to do was to curl up in the corner of the hole, pull her woollen cloak over her face and go to sleep.

The foxes wouldn't let her. When she huddled down, her own little fox with the white tail tip jumped down into the ditch and barked at her, and then pulled on Cassie's cloak with her teeth. She even hissed and Cassie stood up hurriedly, worried that she might nip.

"I won't go to sleep," she promised wearily. The fox cub stood with her, guarding her watchfully, as the other foxes went on digging at the side of the ditch.

At last the foxes retreated and the cub pulled on Cassie's cloak again, dragging her towards the little path they had made. It was still slippery and muddy and hard to climb, but Cassie grabbed on to the grasses, sure this time that if she slid back, the foxes would help her up. She could feel them watching as she slipped and squeaked and scrabbled. Probably they weren't sure why she was so bad at it, she thought as she dragged herself up on to the snow field once more. They could have been out of there in one jump.

"Thank you," she said, blinking hard and trying to see the foxes through the darkness and swirling snow. Four small dark shapes were outlined against the snow – and then three of them slipped away.

"What shall I do now?" Cassie asked the last one, rather helplessly. She needed to walk home but she wasn't sure if she could, now that she was so cold and tired.

The fox beside her was silent and then she let out one sharp warning bark. Cassie peered around, wondering what the fox was worried about. Then she gasped –

there was a light, coming towards them!

"Are you there?" someone called, and Cassie stepped forwards.

"Yes..." she whispered. But she wasn't sure if she was only imagining the light and the voice.

"Did you hear something?" It was a man's voice, low and worried.

"I-I'm here..." Cassie faltered.

"Thank the Lord!" The light came closer, and in its glow Cassie saw an old man and woman, well wrapped up in coats and cloaks. "I told you, Josiah! That was no fox crying, it was a child!" the woman said, surging forward and putting an arm round Cassie's shoulders. "Poor little thing, she's frozen near to death! Where did you come from, sweetling?"

"I was lost – on the river..." Cassie mumbled, her words half swallowed by shivering. "My mother..."

"That Frost Fair, it's no wonder," the woman said wisely. "Such a crowd and all capering about. You come back with us, child, and sit by the fire to warm up.

Your mother must be worried to death. We'll take you back home in the morning, don't fret."

They led Cassie away across the snow, fussing about hot soup and possets with herbs to ward off the cold. But as they came to the door of their cottage, Cassie looked back. A little way behind her, just out of the lantern light, was a fox, watching carefully. And as the old couple drew Cassie inside the fox slipped away and Cassie saw her white tail tip disappear into the snow.

Chapter
EIGHT

Cassie blinked and yawned, and then looked around in confusion. She must have fallen asleep at the kitchen table in the cottage, she thought. She had been drinking warm milk with honey and spices from a thick pottery cup, sipping at it sleepily. The old woman had wrapped a blanket around her shoulders and given her a basin of warm water to help thaw out her cold feet. Sleep had wrapped Cassie up warmer than the blanket, though. She was pretty sure she hadn't finished the milk...

Now she was cold again – leaning against something hard and icy. She sat up, rolling her stiff shoulders and trying to work out where she was. The room was dark and strange, and Cassie's heart began to thump as she tried to see what each odd lumpen shape meant. Then there was a small sound from the corner of the room, a whistling, muttery little sigh, and all at once, Cassie remembered.

She was home. That was Lucas, her baby brother, shifting around in his cot. She was in her own bedroom. She must have gone to sleep sitting on the window seat, leaning against the cold glass and looking at the snow.

But then, the Frost Fair? And the fox, and their journey across the ice? It had happened – she had been there...

Perhaps dreams always felt real. Cassie gulped down a surge of disappointment, a sense that she had lost something precious and strange.

"I made it all up," she whispered to herself. "From talking to Mrs Morris and seeing Frost in the snow."

She frowned. Had that been a dream too, then? Going out of the flat and following the fox cub through the snowy streets? Cassie patted at herself. She was wearing her thick onesie, but not her coat and she didn't have wellies on. Actually, her feet were icy – that was probably what had made her dream about her feet being so cold crossing the frozen river.

She wriggled her toes to try and warm them up a bit, but they still ached. Cassie slid down from the window seat as quietly as she could, thinking that she'd get back into bed and warm up, but then an eerie wailing made her turn around and look out again.

Frost was there, standing in the snow and gazing up at Cassie's window, just as she had been earlier that night – and one night centuries ago. Cassie rubbed her eyes. It was hard to work out what had been a dream and what was real. Outside the little fox was pacing up and down, still letting out those unearthly cries. Cassie had heard the noises before, in the distance, but she had never heard Frost cry like that before. She sounded frightened.

Cassie pressed her hands against the glass and stared down at the fox in the snow, wondering what to do. Frost sounded as though something was desperately wrong, and she was padding back and forth below Cassie's window and wailing. Cassie couldn't leave her there, not crying like that. A strange half memory of a huge dog and a terrified cub made her catch her breath. She had to go down there.

Cassie hurried out into the hallway, listening for her mum. There was a faint sloshing sound from the bathroom – was she still in the bath? Then again, how long had it actually been since Cassie had first gone out? Maybe only minutes. Or perhaps it had never happened at all.

She pulled on thick socks and her

boots, and a coat over her onesie, tucked the spare key in her coat pocket and turned the latch as carefully as she could. Then she sped down the stairs to find the little fox.

As Cassie burst out of the front door, Frost came trotting eagerly towards her, her white-tipped brush swinging. She stood there impatiently, obviously waiting for Cassie to follow her, and then she set off around the back of the building, towards the bin room.

"What is it?" Cassie murmured, glad that at least Frost wasn't leading her off into the streets again. Even though it had been amazing to see the Frost Fair, Cassie didn't think she wanted to go back. Or at least not yet.

Frost stopped and looked round at

Cassie almost triumphantly, as though she had done something very clever.

"But what…" Cassie started to say, and then she realized that there was something in the snow just beyond Frost's paws. A pile of old clothes, it looked like, until Cassie went closer and saw that it was a person, lying there huddled and frozen.

"Mrs Morris!" Cassie yelped, and she crouched down next to the old lady in the snow, gently pulling at her shoulder. "Mrs Morris, are you all right? Did you fall? What happened?"

Mrs Morris didn't answer for a moment and for a horrible second Cassie thought she might not be breathing. But then she turned her head a little and whispered, "You... Cassie?"

"Yes! Are you hurt?"

"I'm not sure. I slipped. My knees... I can't get up."

"I'll get my mum." Cassie patted Mrs Morris's arm. "Don't worry. I won't be a minute." She jumped up and looked at Frost. "Stay here with her," she whispered. "You're so clever. You knew she needed help, didn't you?" Then she leaned over

Mrs Morris again. "Look, don't worry if I'm gone a little while…" and she raced away.

As Cassie dashed back up the stairs, panting, she saw her dad at the door of the flat, just getting out his keys.

"Dad!" she yelled.

"Cassie?" Her dad turned round. "What are you doing out here? It's ten o'clock!"

"I know…" Cassie leaned against the wall, trying to catch her breath. "I heard someone calling and Mum was in the bath, so I went to see what it was." That was actually true, Cassie thought. After all, Frost was someone too. "It's Mrs Morris – she's fallen over in the snow and she can't get up. You have to come and help her!"

"Mrs Morris?" Cassie's dad was already hurrying down the stairs. "I hope she hasn't broken something. How long has she been out there?"

"I don't know." Cassie jumped down the stairs after him. "She wasn't talking when I first found her, but then she woke up a bit. Do you think we ought to call an ambulance?"

"We probably should, if she's been there a while. And it sounds as if maybe she was unconscious." Cassie's dad took in a sharp breath as he saw Mrs Morris lying there in the snow. She looked awfully small, Cassie thought worriedly. Small and fragile.

"Mrs Morris?" he asked gently. "Can you hear me? It's Chris, Cassie's dad, from the flat next door. Can you move at all?"

"I-I don't know..." Mrs Morris's voice was thin and wavery, and Cassie's dad stroked her arm comfortingly.

"Don't worry. Best not to try, I reckon. I'll call an ambulance."

As he stood up and patted his jacket for his phone, Cassie saw a dark shape skitter backwards and disappear into the shadows. Frost had stayed on guard, just as she'd asked.

"Thank you!" Cassie whispered out into the snow.

"When are you coming back home?" Cassie asked. The hospital wasn't as scary as she'd thought it would be, with the flowers and Christmas cards on the table by Mrs Morris's bed, and the other people in the ward chatting to their visitors, but she wouldn't want to have to stay there.

"Soon, they say. Maybe as soon as tomorrow. I didn't even break anything – I was so lucky. They just wanted me to stay in hospital because I'd got so cold," Mrs Morris explained. She smiled at Cassie. "I'm so grateful that you found me! It could have been a lot worse if I'd stayed out in the snow much longer."

"What were you doing out there?"

Mrs Morris sighed. "Taking my rubbish out. And don't tell me it was a stupid thing to do in the snow, Cassie, because I know. Your dad's already told me that and half the doctors in this hospital, I think."

Cassie giggled. "Next time I'll take it down for you, if you like. I wouldn't mind. I do it for Mum."

"Thank you, Cassie." Mrs Morris's eyes sharpened. "And anyway, it's all very well you asking me what *I* was doing out in the snow. Now your mother's gone to change Lucas and we're alone – what were you out there for?"

"I heard you calling," Cassie said glibly. Mum and Dad had believed it, after all.

Mrs Morris frowned. "But I don't think I did call. I should have done, of course.

But I was feeling so strange – sort of dizzy and sick. I didn't shout, Cassie."

"You must have done," Cassie said, pleating the blanket on Mrs Morris's bed between her fingers. "You've just forgotten."

"No." Mrs Morris looked at her thoughtfully and then leaned forward a little. "That isn't the only thing, Cassie. When you went to fetch your dad, you left one of those foxes guarding me."

"What…?" Cassie faltered. She hadn't realized Mrs Morris had heard her.

"One of the young ones," Mrs Morris went on, rather dreamily. "She had a white tip to her tail, like she'd dipped it in paint. She was very pretty, actually. I wasn't scared of her. There were snowflakes on her ears…" Then her gaze sharpened again and she glared at Cassie. "I'm not imagining it, young lady."

Cassie sighed. "No."

"Was it the fox you heard calling, then? Not me?"

Cassie nodded. "She sat outside my window and wailed until I came down."

"And to think I complained about you feeding them, back in the summer," Mrs Morris murmured. "Thank goodness you did. Have you seen her again since?"

"I took her a bit of my breakfast this morning," Cassie admitted. "It was only toast, but she liked it. It had Marmite on."

Mrs Morris laughed. "Well, when I get back, I'll give you another sausage roll. A whole packet, to say thank you." Then she looked at Cassie curiously. "What is it? You look as though you've got a secret, like you're bursting to tell someone."

Cassie stared down at the blanket again. "Would you believe me, if I told you something very strange? Something I'm not even sure really happened, or if it was a dream? Except…"

"Tell me!" Mrs Morris smiled at her. "You don't know how bored I am, lying here. Even if it was only a dream, I'd still like to hear."

"Do you remember telling me about the Frost Fairs?" Cassie swallowed hard. She hadn't told anyone and she wasn't sure what Mrs Morris was going to say.

"Of course. I wasn't sure you really believed me, though."

"Not at first, but then I did, and … and now I know it's true." Cassie looked up at the old lady. "I went there. Frost took me – that's the fox who called me to come and find you."

Mrs Morris shifted a little to sit up more in bed. "What happened?" she asked, frowning curiously.

"Two nights ago, the night you fell. I heard Frost calling, and I went out and followed her. But the streets changed as we were walking and then I was someone else. A girl going to the Frost Fair with her family."

Cassie shook her head. "I decided it must all have been a dream. But then I found this when I was coming here on the bus with Mum. It was in my coat pocket. So now I don't know." She held it out to Mrs Morris and they stared at it together – a little piece of thick paper, crisply printed in black.

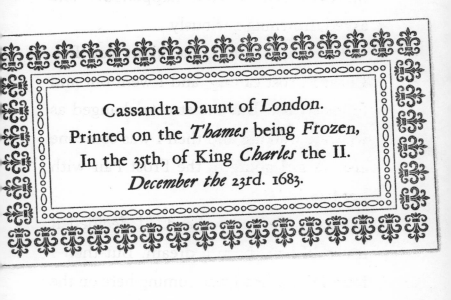

Cassandra Daunt of *London*.
Printed on the *Thames* being Frozen,
In the 35th, of King *Charles* the II.
December the 23rd. 1683.

Turn the page for an extract from

THE STORM DOG

by HOLLY WEBB

Tilly sat at the end of the sofa, looking worriedly at her mum. She was trying to go back through her day at school, wondering if she'd done anything wrong without realizing it that would have made her teacher call home. She couldn't think why else Mum would want to have "a talk" with her just when she'd got back from school.

"You know we're going to Grandma Ellen's house for Christmas?" her mum began slowly.

"Yes! Oh – can't we go?" Tilly slumped a little. "There's nothing wrong with Grandma, is there? Or Great-Gran?" she added, her eyes widening. Great-Gran *was* nearly ninety, even though she was one of the most energetic people Tilly had ever met. She and Tilly's grandma shared a cottage together, and Great-Gran even did most of the gardening.

"Don't panic! It's all fine – we're still going." Mum patted her knee and then sighed. "It's just that there's so much happening at work, I'm not going to be able to take as much time off as I'd planned. I won't be able to go until the day before Christmas Eve."

Tilly made a face. They'd planned to be at Grandma's for a few days before Christmas and she'd been really looking forward to it. There seemed to be more Christmassy things to do there. If they didn't go till the twenty-third, Grandma would have already put up her Christmas tree and Tilly wouldn't get to help decorate it. They only had space for a tiny little tree in their flat and you could hardly fit any decorations on it at all. Maybe Grandma would even put the icing on the Christmas cake without her too…

"That's ages away," she muttered.

Her mum sighed again. "I know. So, I spoke to Grandma earlier on and we were thinking – what if you went up on the train before me?"

"You mean go to Grandma's on my own?" Tilly stared at her mum. She'd never even considered *that*. She'd thought that Mum would say she had to go to holiday club at school again. She'd been just about to moan that holiday club was boring and now Mum had sprung a total surprise on her instead.

"Not for the whole time," her mum hurried to explain. "I'd be coming as soon as I can get off work. I know you love spending time with Grandma Ellen and Great-Gran."

"I do – I mean, I do want to. It's just that I've never been on a train on my own before." Tilly nibbled her bottom lip. Her grandma lived a long way away, in a village close to the Welsh border. It was at least an hour's journey by train. More like an hour and a half.

Her mum nodded. "I know – that's the bit that worries me too, Tilly. I mean, I would put you on the train here and Grandma would meet you at the other end but it's still a big thing to do on your own. No... You're right, it's not going to work. I'll call Grandma later and tell her." She smiled at Tilly. "Don't worry! We'll still get to stay with them for most of Christmas."

Tilly leaned against her mum's shoulder. Could she do it? She went to school on her own now but that was different, it was only a ten-minute walk. She'd been really nervous the first time she did it, though. Perhaps she was making too much fuss about the train? "Don't call Grandma Ellen just yet," she murmured. "I'll … think about it."

"OK. But honestly, Tilly, I don't want you worrying about it." Mum eyed her thoughtfully. "So, did anything interesting happen at school today?"

Tilly sighed heavily. "Guess what Mrs Cole's done." She sat up again, folding her arms and glaring at her mum.

"Um... Given you loads of homework?"

"Worse than that! She's given us a project. To do in the Christmas holidays! It's not fair." Tilly slumped back against the sofa cushions. She'd thought maybe they'd get some spellings over the holidays, or a bit of maths. Not a great big project to do. Everyone in her class was complaining about it.

"What's it on?" Mum asked. "Something interesting?"

"The Second World War." Tilly peered

over at her. "We have to choose a topic, like rationing or something. I suppose it's sort of interesting."

"Oh, it definitely is!" Mum brightened up, tapping her fingers on the sofa as she thought. "You could make some of those weird wartime recipes – I bet we could find them online. Even some Christmassy ones. I'm sure there was a recipe for Christmas pudding with gravy powder in it..."

"Why would I want to make that? It sounds disgusting!" Tilly scrunched up her nose, frowning. "Why would they even *do* that?"

"To make it look the right colour, I think. Because they couldn't get most of the proper ingredients. But you should ask Great-Gran. Actually, Tilly, you could interview her for your project!

You're lucky, I shouldn't think many people in your class have someone in the family to ask."

"I suppose," Tilly agreed doubtfully. She sort of knew that Great-Gran had been a child during the war but she'd never sat down and asked her about it. "Would she mind?"

"I expect she'd love to tell you. We can ask her later when we phone."

Tilly nodded. "I'd better go and do my homework. I'll think about the train, OK?"

Grandma Ellen called Mum anyway, it turned out, just as they were cooking dinner. Tilly stirred the pasta sauce, listening to Mum's half of the conversation.

"Yes, I know. I'd mentioned maybe you could meet her at the station but Tilly's never been on a train on her own before. She's not sure... I'm sorry, we really wanted to come for longer. Oh, OK." Mum waved at Tilly. "Grandma wants to talk to you."

Tilly took the phone. "Hi, Grandma."

"Hello, Tilly love. Don't worry about

the train, we'll work something out. I could come and get you in the car."

Tilly saw Mum start to look worried – she was standing next to Tilly and she could hear Grandma too. "You don't like driving long journeys," she reminded Grandma. "Oh, Mum's waving at me, she wants to talk to you again." Tilly went back to stirring the pasta sauce, hoping that Mum and Grandma wouldn't talk for too much longer. She was getting really hungry. After a few minutes, though, Mum handed her the phone again...

Out now in paperback:

The Snow Cat

Collect them all!

THE SNOW BEAR

FROM BEST-SELLING AUTHOR
HOLLY WEBB

The Reindeer Girl

FROM BEST-SELLING AUTHOR
HOLLY WEBB

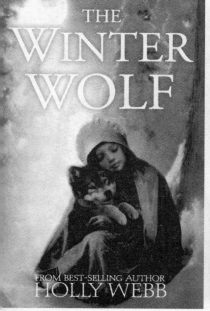

THE WINTER WOLF

FROM BEST-SELLING AUTHOR
HOLLY WEBB

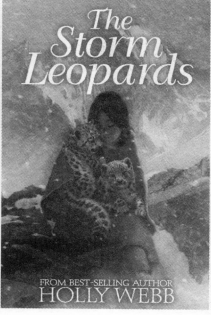

The Storm Leopards

FROM BEST-SELLING AUTHOR
HOLLY WEBB

Also by HOLLY WEBB:

HOLLY WEBB

The HOUNDS of PENHALLOW HALL

THE MOONLIGHT STATUE

Illustrated by
JASON COCKCROFT

HOLLY WEBB

The HOUNDS of PENHALLOW HALL

THE LOST TREASURE

Illustrated by
JASON COCKCROFT

HOLLY WEBB

The HOUNDS of PENHALLOW HALL

THE HIDDEN STAIRCASE

Illustrated by
JASON COCKCROFT

HOLLY WEBB

The HOUNDS of PENHALLOW HALL

THE SECRETS TREE

Illustrated by
JASON COCKCROFT

HOLLY WEBB

Holly Webb started out as a children's
book editor and wrote her first series for
the publisher she worked for. She has been
writing ever since, with over one hundred
books to her name. Holly lives in Berkshire,
with her husband and three young sons.
Holly's pet cats are always nosying around
when she is trying to type on her laptop.

For more information
about Holly Webb visit:

www.holly-webb.com

LON

Please renew or return items by the date
shown on your receipt

www.hertfordshire.gov.uk/libraries

Renewals and enquiries: 0300 123 4049

Textphone for hearing or 0300 123 4041
speech impaired users:

Hertfordshire

L32 11.16

527 823 88 4